Happily, Red

AMY LAURENS

OTHER WORKS

Find other works by the author at
www.amylaurens.com

happily, red

INKLET #11

AMY LAURENS

Inkprint PRESS

www.inkprintpress.com

Print ISBN: 978-1-925825-10-7
eBook ISBN: 9781386798248

www.inkprintpress.com

National Library of Australia Cataloguing-in-Publication Data
Laurens, Amy 1985 –
Happily, Red
24 p.
ISBN: 978-1-925825-10-7
Inkprint Press, Canberra, Australia
1. Fiction—Fantasy—Dark Fantasy 2. Fiction—Short Stories 3. Fiction—Fairy Tales 4. Fiction—Fantasy—Romantic

First Print Edition: June 2019
Cover design © Inkprint Press
Interior art © Amy Laurens

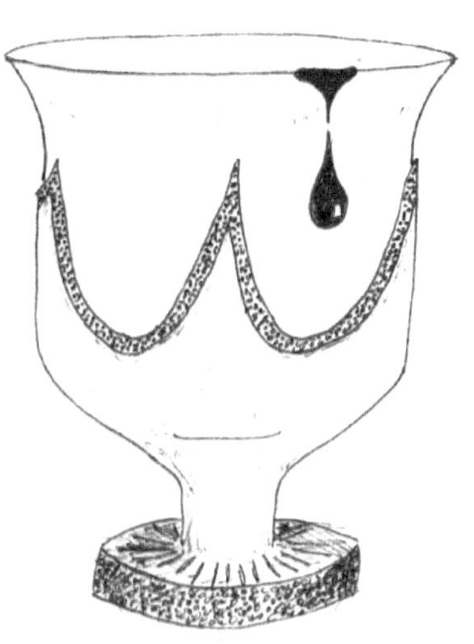

HAPPILY, RED

Occasionally, it is possible to have a happy ending. It's in the bees buzzing officiously around their daisies, the wild lace flowers strewing grass so lush it's thigh-high and crisp, the fresh pinch of early morning air that pinks the cheeks while the glorious golden sunlight promises a warm day; and in the feel of your warm arms around mine.

This doesn't have to be an ending of course. It's also a beginning. Also a middle. Perspective is everything, see.

It would easy to describe the mud stains in the yard, the dead, dull branches on the trees infected with barkbug, the feel of the empty bed beside me when you're gone for days at a time. It would be easy for my mother's words to ring true, to fester in my heart until I was sorry I said yes, until I regretted your smiles and wiles, days spent hand in hand, picnics with scones and clotted cream and fresh-crushed raspberries with sugar.

No. I could never regret those things. Not even on the nights when it feels like you have been gone for a month and I fear you may never return. You know the woods well, and as you saved me once I know that you will save yourself a hundred times—and one day, perhaps, I will save you, though you say I already have.

It is possible to *make* a happy ending.

Perspective, see.

It's in the melody you whistle as you cut across the yard, the gentle werking of the chickens as they bustle in search of grubs, and the flutter of life inside my belly.

It's not that this was my first choice, though the early springtime air and the smell of baking apples isn't far from heaven.

Let's face it: if I'd have chosen, I'd have chosen not to need rescuing in the first place. I'd have chosen...

But no. There's no way to replay things that doesn't leave one of my family dead, me or grandmother, or maybe even you.

That there was anything left to save is a happy ending of its own—and of course, that's where the stories usually end. But for those of us that must live it, life doesn't end just because the monster's slain. Even when the monster leaves a special gift behind.

For Mother, it was an end.

She'd have rathered me dead.

But you... As you pause to smile at me over the furry backs of our goats, my heart flutters in time with the kicks in my belly, and I know that you believe in hope, in new beginnings. That's why I'm with you, in the end.

Not because you saved me from the belly of the wolf, and not because you save me from the curses of the moon that the wolf so generously bestowed, but because you believed that despite it all, I could be happy. That's a power all its own, you know.

You're coming towards the house now, my red cloak slung casually round your neck. It means nothing to you, that symbol of blood, of horror, of innocences lost. I love you for that.

The blood you bring me, still warm from the veins of the wolf it ran in, tastes good: sharp and iron-like. But I wouldn't drink it at all if it weren't for the glimmer in your eyes that offers laughter when I'm done, the utter lack of judgement as you bid me drink my tonic. If it weren't for that, I'd never drink; I'd gladly lose myself in fur and fangs and lack of thought.

Mother's ending wasn't worth living for.

Yours...

A happy ending's always possible. You just have to carve the path.

Thank you for believing. For you, for hope, I'll drink the wolf's blood forever. Hope is the most powerful tonic of all, and who knows how long this happy ending might last.

Happily,
Red

THE MAKING OF
HAPPILY, RED

I have a feeling it was one of those days—you know the ones. The ones where everybody is debating what makes 'Literature', and the English faculties are firmly divided as to whether happy endings have any literary merit at all, or whether we can only learn from the gloomy things in life.

I think you can guess which camp I live in. I'll give you a hint: it's in the first line of this story.

I didn't set out to write a great piece of Literature with a happy ending just to prove everyone wrong; in fact, I didn't really set out to do anything in particular with this story. I just knew that I wanted to assert, in some small way, the possibility—and plausibility—of happiness as an ending in and of itself. The plot, such as it is, spiralled in from there.

Oh yes. I did have one other thing in mind: this saying. It's one of my favourites.

Everything's okay in the end. If it's not okay, it's not the end.

DOWNLOAD YOUR FREE EBOOK

When you buy a print book from Inkprint Press, we like to say THANK YOU by offering you the ebook for free!

Please head to
www.inkprintpress.com/inklets/11/
and the use the coupon INK11 to get your copy of this Inklet in epub AND mobi today!
(Coupon will only work once.)

Read more by Amy Laurens!

F O R   A   L I T T L E
W H I L E :
I N   T H E   E V E N I N G ,
W H E R E   T H E
D E S E R T S   E N D

In the evening, when my heart
is as full as the sky is of stars,
then I will go out to the dunes of
sand that stretch endlessly to the sea,
and
there I will wait.
In the sparkling
starlight of the night, I will wait
for you,
and when you come we will leap
hand in hand
down slopes that fall away under our
feet until
we can fly,
and together we will soar

through the night like bats,
great, leathery wings of belief
pinning us to the sky.
We will dip and twist and glide and
turn, and
when we have flown high enough,
                    your hand clenched
tightly in mine like we are locked
           together eternally,
we will reach the stars.
The dunes will stretch below us like a
sea,
waves of sand frozen in place only
by time and perspective, and
we will see that the boundaries of our
                              desert
are finite;
that the barrenness of our minds
comes to
an end;
and that outside it all is fertile.
Together
we will swoop back to the ground
           and remember

what we have seen from our vantage
point of the stars: we will walk
onwards
with steps that achingly climb, only to
slip
back halfway to where they came from,
and
our muscles will burn
as we scale the heights of our
disappointments
—but we will not forget.
We have been to the stars,
and they have shown us:
the desert too will
end.

One day, we will find the fence, and
scale it.

ABOUT THE AUTHOR

AMY LAURENS is an Australian author of fantasy fiction for all ages. Her comic fantasy series, *Kaditeos: Mercury*, follows Mercury's misadventures as she tries to take over the capital of Kaditeos, complete with a ferret. She has also written the *Sanctuary* series, a portal-fantasy trilogy set in Australia, for readers aged 10 and up.

As well as fiction, Amy has also written several entries in the *Inkprint Writers* series on using theme in stories (and how to figure out the theme of a story), on writing about dogs, and on the many ways that climate influences culture.

You can find out more about Amy at her website, www.amylaurens.com.

INKLETS

Collect them all! Released on the 1st and 15th of each month.

INKLET #007
SEVENTY
LIANA BROOKS

INKLET #008
A Final Request for Mercy
AMY LAURENS

INKLET #009
the kitten psychologist vs. the kitten's owners
THEA VAN DIEPEN

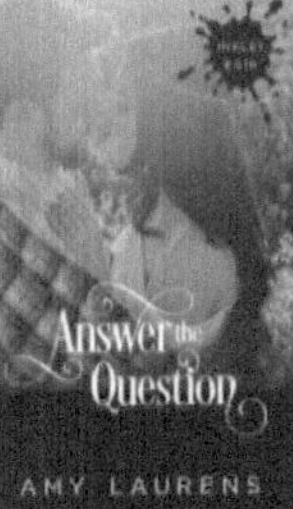
Answer the Question
AMY LAURENS

Happily, Red
AMY LAURENS

INKLET #012
the kitten psychologist tries to be patient through email
THEA VAN DIEPEN

DRAGON Tuesday
AMY LAURENS

RED PLANET REFUGEES
LIANA BROOKS

the kitten psychologist & What The Kitten Did
THEA VAN DIEPEN

INKLET #016
Cherry Blossom
AMY LAURENS

INKLET #017
Alone
AMY LAURENS

INKLET #018
the kitten psychologist
& The Kitten
Come To A Conclusion
THEA VAN DIEPEN

INKLET #019
LEVEL NINE
LIANA BROOKS

INKLET #020
To Dust
AMY LAURENS

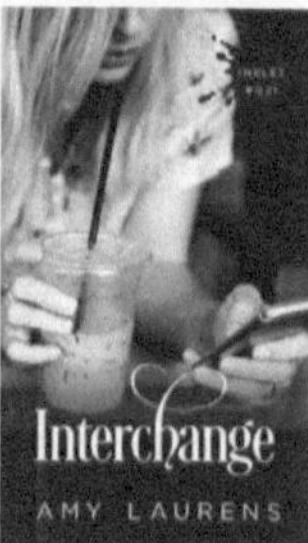

INKLET #021
Interchange
AMY LAURENS

INKLET #022
Emalia's Lanterns
LIANA BROOKS

INKLET #023
Dear Santa
AMY LAURENS

INKLET #024
The Quilt-Maker's Scrap
AMY LAURENS